CONTENTS

CHAPTER 1

NEW SEASON, NEW COACH

Mia Hernandez started her warm-ups before she reached the gym. As she walked to the gymnastics training centre from her home, she jogged, pranced with pointed toes and power skipped.

She didn't care if people driving past her thought she looked odd. She wanted to fight off the chill in the

November air and get her muscles working. Plus she needed to be ready to jump into the first practice of the new season with her teammates.

When Mia reached the training centre, her home away from home, she quickly took off her joggers and hoodie. Underneath she wore her red leotard and black shorts. She slipped off her trainers and socks, and pulled her long, curly brown hair into a high ponytail.

As she walked barefoot to the floor exercise mat, she raised her head to look at the large banner on the wall. It read *Home of the Ridgefield Rams, Middle School State Champions.*

Mia took her first gymnastics class in this gym when she was five years old. Eight years later, she was a key member of the Ridgefield Rams, and they were hoping to continue their winning streak.

On the mat, Mia stood next to her best friend, Riley, and joined her in doing some stretches.

"Just starting?" asked Mia.

Mia and Riley stood with their feet shoulder-width apart.

"Yeah," said Riley.

They each did eight backward swings with their right arms and then switched to do eight on the left side.

"I already did my cardio warm-up," said Riley.

"I did mine on the way over," said Mia.

After arm swings, the girls started trunk twists.

"Do your neighbours think something is wrong with you when they see you prancing instead of walking normally?"

"No, they're used to it," Mia said with a laugh. She often did cartwheels or leaps while walking with her parents and their Jack Russell terrier called Split.

The girls leaned into deep lunges, toes pointed forwards, back legs straight.

"Are you nervous about this season?" Riley asked.

Mia assumed Riley was talking about her uneven bars routine. Mia was confident and competent on every gymnastics apparatus, except for the uneven bars.

Each time she practised or competed, she feared she would balk and hurt herself, like she did in the sixth grade.

"I'm always nervous about the bars," Mia said.

"I didn't mean that," said Riley. She gave Mia a sympathetic look. "I meant because we're the defending champions."

Mia laughed, a little embarrassed. "Of course," she said. "Getting to the top was hard. Staying there will probably be harder. This year, we're the ones to beat."

"Right," said Riley. "Plus, we have a new coach. That could change everything."

"Exactly," said Mia. "Hey, look. Here she comes."

The girls stopped stretching as soon as they saw their new coach walking towards them. She wore black leggings and a blue and gold Ridgefield Rams T-shirt. Her blonde hair was in a tight French plait. The other girls also stopped what they were doing and gathered on the floor exercise mat to meet their new coach.

"Hello, girls. I'm Coach Taylor," she paused and smiled.

Mia shifted her weight from one foot to the other. She looked at her teammates. Everyone seemed a bit nervous.

"I'm really excited to be here. I'm also a little nervous," said Coach Taylor. "I know I've got big shoes to fill. It's okay if you're nervous too. Getting a new coach isn't easy. Coach Bennett is an amazing person and teacher. I'm sure it was hard for you all to see her go."

Mia let out a deep breath. She felt better knowing that her new coach understood how they were feeling.

"I think you'll feel more at ease knowing that I was once a gymnast at Brookfield Middle School," said Coach Taylor.

Mia and Riley exchanged surprised looks. Allison Perez, an eighth-grader, booed. Some girls laughed nervously.

Coach Taylor smiled and held up her hands. "I guess I should have expected that. I know they're your biggest rivals."

"But, you see," Coach continued, "I have first-hand experience with them. I know how they're trained. The current Brookfield coach was my coach."

"Well that might be useful," Allison said.

Coach nodded. "The ancient Chinese general Sun Tzu said, 'Know thy enemy and know yourself; in a hundred battles, you will never be defeated.'" Coach smirked when she said, "I know our enemy."

After a moment, she added, "And I will get to know each of you. My insider information, plus your hard work, will make us unbeatable." Coach pounded a fist into her palm for emphasis.

Mia looked at Riley and then glanced at her other teammates again. Everyone looked much less worried.

"If we're going to defend our title, then we'd better get to work," said Coach Taylor.

Coach led the girls through star jumps, high frog leaps and more stretching. Then she split everyone up and instructed them to run through their old routines.

"Today, I will mostly observe and take notes. I want to learn our strengths and see where we can improve." Coach read names from her clipboard, assigning each girl to a station.

Please send me to floor exercise first, Mia pleaded in her head. *I want to start the first practice on a positive note.*

"Mia?"

Mia snapped back to the moment. She hadn't realized Coach had said something to her. "I'm sorry. What did you say?"

"Mia, I'd like you to start on the uneven bars."

CHAPTER 2

FAITH AND PHYSICS

Mia's stomach was in knots as she jogged to her duffel bag, which she had left against a wall. She unzipped her bag and fished out her wristbands and hand grips.

Mia's mum had bought her a new blue grip bag with her name embroidered in gold on one side and "You've got this!" on the other.

That's right, Mia thought to herself, seeing the words *I've got this.*

She slid on her wristbands. Then she strapped on her hand grips as she walked towards the uneven bars.

I've been getting better and stronger each year, Mia reminded herself. *I've landed on my feet countless times since I fell in sixth grade. I can do this.*

She was jolted out of her mental pep talk when Allison walked up behind her.

"Bawk!" Allison chirped like a chicken in Mia's ear. She had been doing this ever since Mia's uneven bar disaster.

"Allison, knock it off already!" said Mia. "Your joke is two years old. It's not funny! It was never funny!"

Mia's cheeks warmed from anger and embarrassment. *Why won't she let it go?*

Looking around the gym, Mia realized her teammates were watching her snap at Allison. Coach Taylor also noticed and quickly walked towards the girls.

"What's going on?" asked Coach Taylor.

"Nothing," said Mia.

"It clearly was something," said Coach.

"Fine," said Allison. "I bawked at Mia. You know, like a chicken. *Bawk-bawk*." She flapped her elbows to demonstrate.

"O-kay," said Coach Taylor, slowly, emphasizing each syllable. "And why are you making chicken sounds at Mia?"

"Because in the sixth grade, I balked during a bars routine," said Mia. "I was working on my first salto backward straight dismount. When I wasn't practising, I was watching every video I could find. Plus Coach Bennett taught me about faith and physics."

"Faith and physics?" asked Coach Taylor.

"A body in motion stays in motion," said Mia. "We have to follow through with the motion. If we freeze, we fall. She also said we have to have faith in ourselves after all of our hard work."

"Faith and physics. I like that," said Coach Taylor. "So, what went wrong?"

"I lacked faith, and because of that, I violated the first rule of physics," said Mia. "I didn't commit to the move. I launched myself but didn't go into the rotation. I halted the motion and flailed in the air until I landed face-down on the mat."

"Were you hurt?" asked Coach.

"I cracked a rib," said Mia. She shrugged. "It could have been much worse. I mean, I have fallen lots of times. That's part of learning, but this was in competition."

Allison rolled her eyes. "This is the longest story ever. Have you finished?"

Mia ignored her. "I balked, so, she bawked at me. Get it?"

"I've got it," said Coach.

She crossed her arms over her chest and sighed. She was about to say something when Mia spoke again.

"And it wasn't once or twice. She bawks at me all the time. It's annoying." Mia then looked directly at Allison and said, "*You're* annoying."

"Whoa, girls," said Coach. "Let's all take a deep breath."

"Sorry, Coach, but I've been dealing with this for two years," said Mia. "I've been working hard to get over what happened, and she keeps rubbing it in my face."

"Lighten up," said Allison. "Did you ever think that maybe I'm trying to encourage you?"

"How is bawking at me encouraging?" Mia demanded.

"We lost that day because of you," said Allison.

"I know," said Mia. "You don't need to keep reminding me."

"Well, I hate to lose," said Allison, "so, I'm reminding you that fear leads to losing. One slip-up costs us first place. We're state champions this year. We can't afford to freeze in mid-air."

"I know that," said Mia. "I'm not buying that you're trying to encourage me. You're trying to intimidate me. You want to mess with my head so that you have a better chance of winning individual events, especially on bars."

Allison shook her head. "I don't need to intimidate you to beat you, Mia."

"Okay, I've heard enough," said Coach. "First of all, we're all on the same team. I know there's competition among teammates. Believe me, I went through the same thing when I was a school athlete. We fought to qualify for all-around and event finals. We also battled to be captain in our senior year. It got nasty – *really* nasty. Even when you're on a team, you seek individual glory. I get that."

Coach turned to Allison and said, "I *hate* to lose too. Seriously, I despise it. I expect us to win every competition, no matter what. But bawking at Mia isn't helping her. If your goal was to encourage her –"

"Yeah, right," Mia interrupted.

Coach put her hand up to Mia. "If your goal was to encourage her, as you said, then it's not working. You need to stop this chicken act right now."

"Fine," said Allison.

"Mia, now that Allison has agreed to stop bawking, I want you to let this go," Coach said. "You need to support each other. Also, you both need to set an example. You're eighth-graders. The younger girls look up to you."

Mia and Allison glanced round the gym. Coach was right. The other girls were trying to practise but kept looking over at them, distracted by the drama.

"Fine," said Mia.

"Good," said Coach. "Let's focus on crushing other teams instead of fighting among ourselves."

Mia and Allison nodded.

"Now, Mia, show me your old routine," said Coach. "I'd like to see your faith and physics in action."

Mia mentally ran through her routine as she

double-checked her hand grips and chalked up. When she was ready, she faced the low bar. She took one more deep breath and then jumped forwards.

She gripped the lower bar, completed a glide kip, and pushed herself into a handstand. Her body came back around, doing another glide kip, but this time she completed a stoop through and reached for the top bar.

As soon as she gripped the top bar, she did another kip cast to a handstand and then two clear hip circles into handstands. Mia did her first giant circle backwards into a one-hundred-and-eighty-degree turn in a handstand.

Next came three backward giant circles with straddled legs. With each full swing around, she gained momentum in preparation for her dismount.

The bar squeaked as the weight of her body circled round it. The air whooshed in her ears as she picked up speed.

A body in motion stays in motion, Mia thought to

herself. *Stay in motion. Commit to the move. If you freeze, you fall. Have faith. You've got this.*

As Mia came around the final time, she let her hands go and flipped her body once all the way round. Her legs were stuck together and perfectly straight. Her toes were pointed. She landed on the mat with a thud and stuck the landing. A perfect salto backward straight – the same dismount that scared her two years ago.

"Go, Mia!" shouted Riley from across the gym.

"Great job, Mia!" said Coach Taylor. "I love that you've mastered the skill that once terrified you."

"Thanks!" said Mia.

"Actually, it almost looks too easy for you now," said Coach. "You've got some complicated moves in your routine, but then you end with a low-level dismount."

Mia's stomach sank. *I know where this is going, and I don't like it.*

"Let's plan to add a more difficult dismount,"

said Coach. "It will be a good personal challenge for you, and it will help the team in competitions. A higher-level move earns more points."

"True," Mia said reluctantly.

"How about we add a twist to your backward straight? Or you can try a double salto backward tucked, or a double salto backward pike," said Coach.

"If she's upping her dismount, I will too," said Allison. "You know, a little friendly competition."

Mia shot Allison a hard stare.

At the end of practice, Mia told Riley what had happened.

"Doing one full rotation was hard enough. Now she wants me to add a twist or do two full backward tucks?" said Mia. "And of course Allison wants to outdo my every move."

"I'm sorry," said Riley. "I know learning a new dismount will be hard. Coach is right, though. Harder routines will be good for the team."

"I know," said Mia. "It's just . . . I was so looking

forward to our new season. Now I feel like there's a

big cloud hanging over it."

CHAPTER 3

A MUSICAL MISTAKE

Mia and her teammates practised for two hours, three days a week. Mia had been practising her new dismount. She decided to try the double salto backward tuck since the move was similar to one she did in her floor exercise routine.

But Mia wasn't ready to show off her new dismount at Saturday's competition at Mayfield. She spent her time in practice mastering the move, but she often landed on the crash pads instead of on her feet.

"Don't worry," Coach Taylor told her. "You'll be ready by the state finals, which is when it will matter most."

Coach Bennett used to take the bus with the team to other schools. Coach Taylor, though, said she would drive. She wanted to get there early to make sure she had everything organized.

As soon as the Ridgefield Rams school bus arrived at Mayfield Middle School, the girls scrambled down the steps and made their way to the locker room. The girls quickly removed their coats and layers of clothes over their team leotards. Their leotards were royal blue with yellow-gold rhinestones around the scoop neck and the cuffs of the sleeves.

Mia looked in the mirror to make sure that every wisp of hair was slicked down and away from her face. All of the girls agreed to wear something yellow in their hair. Some laced yellow ribbons through their French plaits, while others used yellow hair ties to secure their ponytails. Mia's hair was tightly wound in a bun secured with a yellow scrunchie.

Once her hair was perfect, Mia checked her drawstring bag to make sure she had everything she needed: water bottle, wristbands, grip bag, deodorant, snacks and athletic tape.

She hooked her arms through the bag's straps and then looked at Riley.

"Ready?" asked Mia.

"So ready," said Riley. She then raised her voice and said, "Let's go and get our first win!"

The team cheered and walked into the gym, one behind the other. After warm-ups, the girls were split into groups and sent to their first events. With sixteen girls on each team, a group of Rams went to the vault and another went to the beam. A group of Mayfield Hornets went to the bars and another went to floor exercise. Each group competed at the same time and then rotated to the next event.

Mia, Riley and Allison were among the Rams who started on the vault. While Mia waited for her turn, she ran through each move in her head. She also cheered on her teammates, even Allison. As Coach said, they were on the same team and needed to support each other.

When it was Mia's turn, she stood next to the run and waited for the judge's signal that they were ready for her. When the judge raised his hand, Mia stepped onto the run and lifted her arms to show she was ready and about to begin. She hopped on her toes once and then took off.

She raced down the padded runway. Her arms pumped hard to help fuel her powerful stride. When she approached the springboard, she turned slightly and put her hands on the pad. She kicked her legs into a roundoff that ended with her feet landing on the springboard.

The move propelled her body backwards towards the vault. Her hands came down onto the top of the vault. She pushed herself up and out as her legs came around twice, straight and together, before she landed on the mat. Her feet planted in the spot. No steps or wobbles. She threw her hands in the air to signal she had finished.

Her teammates clapped and cheered – even Allison – as she walked back to the start of the run to do it again. Afterwards, Mia paced nervously as she waited for her score. When her 9.7 was posted, she let out the breath she was holding in and high-fived her teammates.

Now she could relax. She only had to watch and cheer on her teammates until everyone had finished and they could rotate to the next event. Between runs, Mia looked around the gym to watch the other events. A girl from the Mayfield team was in her ready position for her floor exercise routine.

When the music started, the girl sprang into action. A second later, she stopped and shook her head. Her coach ran to the judge's table to say something. After a minute, the coach signalled to the girl to start again. She got ready and the music started. She began her routine, and then stopped again. She shook her head in frustration and swiped at tears in her eyes.

I know that feeling. Tears of frustration, not sadness, thought Mia.

Riley came up next to Mia.

"What's going on?"

"I think the wrong music keeps playing," Mia said.

"Oh, no!" said Riley.

"I know," said Mia. "Any little thing can throw off your concentration."

Allison joined the girls. "It shouldn't," she said. "She should be able to go on, no matter what."

"Yeah, but floor exercise is choreographed to music," said Mia. "Having the music makes a difference."

The Mayfield coach signalled for the girl to try a third time.

"See, I told you," said Allison. "Her coach wants her to keep going."

For a third time, the music started, but it was the wrong song.

"What the heck?" asked Riley.

"Yeah, where are the sound techs? This shouldn't happen," said Mia.

This time, the gymnast performed her routine without music. People in the stands and other gymnasts clapped in a steady rhythm to provide a beat and encourage the gymnast as she tumbled.

Mia and Riley joined in the clapping. Allison did not.

At the end of the girl's routine, she didn't rotate fully on a back tuck and fell forwards. She landed on her hands and knees. She stayed there for a few moments, frozen. Finally, her coach went to her side, bent over and whispered something in her ear.

The girl nodded. She stood up and raised her arms, signalling the end of her routine. She walked off the mat with tears running down her face and her coach by her side.

"Wow," said Mia. "I feel so sorry for her."

"I don't," said Allison.

"What is wrong with you?" asked Mia. "You don't care about anyone but yourself."

"What? I'm not trying to be mean," said Allison.

"Right, you don't have to try. It's natural for you."

"Whatever," said Allison. "My point is things go wrong all the time. Serious competitors keep going."

"Well, she did go through with the routine," Riley pointed out.

"Right, so she will get a score instead of no score. That's a plus for them," said Allison. "But she fell at the end, so that's a wrap."

"Not necessarily," said Mia.

"You say there's something wrong with me, but you're the one rooting for the other team."

"I'm not rooting for them," said Mia. "I'm just saying they had one bad performance."

"Right," said Allison. "One slip-up can cost a team first place. You know all about that, right, Mia? Oh, sorry. I'm not supposed to remind you about that."

Mia didn't answer. She crossed her arms over her chest and gave Allison her best glare.

"The reality is that girl's floor exercise routine just put the whole Mayfield team at a disadvantage," said Allison. "As long as we do our best, we win today. Stop feeling sorry for the competition and focus."

As Allison walked away, Mia shook her head. "I know Coach wants us to support each other, but she makes it so hard," she said.

"You have to support her as a teammate," Riley said. "You don't have to like her or be best friends. Besides, you already have an awesome best friend." Riley smiled wide and they both laughed. "Don't let her get to you."

"I'll try," said Mia, "but that's easier said than done."

CHAPTER 4

ADJUST AND CONTINUE

At the next team practice, the girls talked about their first victory as they stretched. They also talked about what happened with the Mayfield gymnast's music.

"How could that happen?" asked Riley. "Don't they have people in charge of the music? Like, isn't that their one job?"

Mia and her teammates laughed.

"Well, yes, they have tech people," said Coach Taylor, "but anything can go wrong. People make mistakes. Technology doesn't always work. It happens."

"So you think it was an accident?" asked Allison.

Everyone was quiet for a moment.

Coach Taylor blinked wildly as if she'd been caught off guard. "You don't think it was a technological glitch?" she asked.

Allison shrugged. "Who knows? At the 2000 Olympics the vault was set two inches too low. It messed everyone up. That could have been a mistake, but maybe not."

"You need to stop watching crime dramas," Mia said.

"Oh, so the girl who doesn't like jokes actually has jokes," said Allison.

"Ladies, that's enough," said Coach Taylor. "I don't know what happened with the music, but the lesson to be learned from the Mayfield competition is that we need to be ready for anything," said Coach Taylor. "You never know when something will happen that is outside of your control. You also never know when someone might try to purposely throw you off."

"So, do you think Allison is right?" asked Mia. "Do you think someone messed with the music on purpose?"

"I don't know," said Coach Taylor. "Maybe. It's definitely possible."

Coach Taylor sneered and looked lost in thought for a moment. "Actually, strange things happened when I was on the Brookfield team."

"Really? What happened?" asked Mia.

"Once, when we competed against Mayfield, the lights went out," said Coach.

The girls gasped.

"I know," said Coach. "Someone could have been seriously hurt. And when we competed against Town Ridge, someone set off the fire alarm."

The girls shook their heads and mumbled to each other.

"Did someone do those things on purpose to mess up the athletes?" asked Riley.

Coach nodded. "No one could prove it," said Coach. "But, yeah, I'm sure of it."

Mia and Riley looked at each other with shocked expressions.

"How do you know that?" asked Allison.

Coach waved a hand and said, "Forget it. I don't want to rehash the past or worry you girls. It is possible that what happened to Mayfield was a simple technical error that couldn't be corrected in the moment. The takeaway is that we need to be prepared to compete regardless of what's thrown at us. We should be able to adjust and continue, no matter what."

"That's exactly what I said," said Allison. She gave Mia an "I told you so" look.

"With that in mind, we are going to practise our floor exercise routines with no music," said Coach.

"Then, I am going to play random songs so you can practise improvisation."

Some girls groaned and others laughed.

"You will need to adjust in the moment and continue your routine," Coach said. "This will be good practice in case something goes wrong with your music during a competition."

During her turn, Mia imagined every beat in her mind. She moved through her routine with grace and power. Performing with no music was easy. She had been trained to mentally run through her moves, with or without the actual music playing.

On her first tumbling pass, she did a front tuck followed by a roundoff, back handspring, back tuck. The parts in between the tumbling passes needed music the most. The body rolls and hip shakes looked a little silly without the music.

When it was Riley's turn, the music started, but then it cut out.

"No!" Riley shouted.

"Adjust and continue," said Coach Taylor. "Hear the music in your head and keep moving."

Riley stumbled through the moves a bit but then refocused and got back into a groove. She finished her routine without any major mistakes.

"Great!" said Coach when she was done. "Now it's Allison's turn."

Allison got into her ready position. When the music started, it wasn't hers at all – just like what happened at the competition against Mayfield. Allison blinked hard but started her routine. By the look on Allison's face, Mia could see that she was trying to match her rhythmic moves with the new music.

Halfway through the routine, the music changed again – to a fast-paced country song that was totally not Allison's style.

"Not fair, Coach!" Allison shouted.

"Adjust and continue," Coach responded.

Allison kicked her legs out side-to-side like an amateur square dancer, which made everyone laugh.

"Now, that's funny!" shouted Mia.

When the music stopped, Coach Taylor said, "It wasn't easy, right?"

"Doing the routine with no music was probably easier than having it change in the middle," said Allison.

Mia agreed with her, but she couldn't help but snap back at Allison. "Of course, whatever you do is most difficult," said Mia.

"Ladies, please," said Coach. She held up her hands like stop signals. "Each of you faced a different challenge and you worked through it. You adjusted and continued. You completed your routine, which, in the end, helps your team in competition."

They were all quiet for a moment.

"Adjust and continue," said Coach. "Let me hear you say it."

"Adjust and continue!" they repeated.

"No matter what," added Coach.

"No matter what!" the team shouted back.

CHAPTER 5

A HARMFUL PRANK

The next competition was against Town Ridge Middle School. After warm-ups, Mia, Allison and Riley were among the Rams assigned to floor exercise as their first event. After practising with no music, Mia was sure she could adjust and continue to whatever might come her way.

Mia and her teammates were still getting settled when they heard girls shouting at both the beam and uneven bars.

"What on earth is going on?" asked Coach, who was standing near by.

Girls from the Town Ridge team were scratching at the palms of their hands and the bottoms of their feet. Many of the girls wiped their hands on the fronts of their thighs to rid their hands of the chalk, but this caused them to claw at their legs too.

"I'll be right back," said Coach. She ran across the floor exercise mat to the judges and then ran over to Town Ridge's coaches and assistant coaches. After a brief, tense-looking conversation, Coach Taylor returned.

"What's going on, Coach?" asked Mia.

"They think some kind of itching powder was put into the chalk bins," said Coach Taylor.

Mia and Riley gasped, but Allison laughed.

"Allison!" said Mia. "You have such a warped sense of humour. Seriously. This is not funny."

"Mia's right, Allison," said Coach. "We need to be respectful during competitions."

"Sorry, Coach," said Allison. "But it's itching powder. It's harmless. Someone is obviously pulling a prank on us."

Coach shrugged. Mia noticed that Coach also slightly curled her lips, like she was trying not to smile or laugh a little bit.

Mia smiled a little then too. *Maybe it is just a harmless prank,* she thought.

Mia and her teammates watched as the itchy Town Ridge girls wiped their bodies with wet towels. Others ran into the locker room to wash off the chalk. One girl who was coated in white powder started to sneeze. She bent over and put her hands on her knees. She then fell forward and rolled onto her back. Her coach ran to her side and put her ear up to the girl's lips to hear what she was trying to say.

The girl's parents scrambled down the stands and ran across the gym to get to their daughter's side. The girl's mother pulled her into a sitting position and put an asthma inhaler to the girl's mouth. The girl sucked in the medicine, but immediately started gagging, coughing and wheezing. It looked like the inhaler was not helping her to breathe easier.

Frantic, the girl's coach stood up and waved her arms. She shouted, "She can't breathe! She's having an asthma attack! Call 9-1-1!"

Mia and her teammates were stunned and silent as they watched the scene unfold. Mia was embarrassed that she had smiled about this at all, that she thought for a second that the itching powder was a funny practical joke.

"Do you still think it's a harmless prank?" Mia asked Allison.

Allison shook her head and looked concerned.

"What should we do, Coach?" asked Riley.

"There's nothing we can do but wait," said Coach Taylor, whose face was pale. She crossed her arms tightly across her chest and paced back and forth.

The ambulance arrived within minutes. Paramedics entered the gym, and the Town Ridge gymnast was soon carried out and taken to the hospital. Officials cleared away all of the chalk bins and stands. They replaced them with new, clean bins. They also brought out brand-new buckets of chalk to prove to everyone that the powder was fresh.

One of the judges then came over the loudspeaker.

"Attention, everyone. First, I want to apologize to everyone for what happened. We will be investigating this to see if we can identify the person who tainted the chalk and put at least one girl's health at risk. Second, I want to thank you for being patient while we tended to the Town Ridge gymnasts. We talked to the Town Ridge coaches. They said the girls are definitely rattled . . ." The announcer paused.

"Do you think they'll forfeit?" asked Mia.

"They're losers if they do," said Allison.

"Girls, please be quiet!" said Coach.

They all turned their attention back to the official making the announcement.

The announcer continued, "But they have decided to continue with the competition."

Everyone in the gym clapped.

"Since the gymnasts have been sitting and waiting for a while, we are going to allow everyone to run through warm-ups again before we officially begin," the announcer concluded.

Coach Taylor let out a heavy sigh. She turned towards the girls and said, "Adjust and continue. You heard her. Go out and warm up. Clear your heads and get ready to compete."

* * *

On the bus ride back to Ridgefield Middle School, the girls were quiet despite their win. Celebrating seemed wrong after what had happened to the Town Ridge team.

Mia sat in the last seat with Riley, far away from Allison. Still, Mia whispered as she spoke because she only wanted her best friend to hear her.

"I think the music issue at the first meet and the itching powder today are related," said Mia.

"You do?" asked Riley. "You don't think the music mess-up was an honest mistake or technical problem?"

"I would have, if that was the only thing that happened," said Mia. "After what happened today, I can't help but think someone is purposely sabotaging the other teams."

"Who would do that?" asked Riley.

"Allison," said Mia without hesitation.

"Come on, Mia. I know you guys don't get along, and she's definitely got an edge to her. But do you really think she would go out of her way to do those things?"

"It doesn't take much to mess up the music or add itching powder to the bins," said Mia. "All she would have to do is push some buttons on the music console or throw some powder into the chalk bins as she walked by. It's so easy. People are crisscrossing the gym all the time. It would be hard to spot someone doing it."

"I don't know, Mia."

"Plus, she has that sick sense of humour. She thought it was funny and harmless," said Mia. She swallowed hard, embarrassed again because she thought that, too, for a moment.

"At first," said Riley. "But then she seemed upset that the Town Ridge gymnast had such a bad reaction."

"Well, maybe that proves she has a conscience when she goes too far," said Mia. "Plus, Allison hates to lose. She said so herself."

"Nobody likes to lose," said Riley. "I don't like to lose, but that doesn't mean I'm going to sabotage other teams. That's next-level stuff, Mia."

"I know," said Mia. "And I think Allison is capable

of next-level stuff. She's got the temper and nasty attitude. She booed Coach Taylor at the first practice. She bawked at me for two whole years. She had zero sympathy for the Mayfield girl when her music cut out. Today, she laughed when the girls were scratching their skin raw."

"Well, when you lay it out like that, it makes sense," said Riley. "But what should we do? Should we say something to Coach?"

"I don't know," said Mia. "We have no evidence. If I say something, Coach might think I'm accusing Allison just because I don't like her."

"True," said Riley.

"I guess all we can do is watch her closely from now on," said Mia. "Maybe she will do or say something that will prove it."

CHAPTER 6

TRUST EXERCISES

Mia shuffled her feet through light, fluffy snow as she walked the four blocks to the gymnastics training centre. She didn't jog or prance with pointed toes, like she did at the start of the season. Her emotions rose and dipped after what happened at the meet against Town Ridge.

One minute, she was energised and determined to prove that Allison was behind it all. The next minute, she was depressed and angry that one person's need to win was ruining her team's whole season.

Mia entered the training centre and stamped the flakes from her boots. Then she headed to the locker room. She shoved what she could into a tiny locker and piled the rest of her belongings under one of the benches.

A minute later, Allison walked in, pulling her hair into a ponytail.

"Hi," said Allison.

"Hi," said Mia.

Mia was almost ready to leave, but now she wanted to hang around. Maybe she could get Allison to say something that proved she was guilty.

Mia pulled her hair tie out, shook her curls loose, and started again.

"Was your mobile phone blowing up over the weekend?" asked Mia.

"Why?" asked Allison. She took off her winter coat and shoved it into a locker.

"Just curious," said Mia. "You know, because of what happened at the Town Ridge competition."

"Well, yeah, my friends and family kept texting me. They wanted to know what happened," said Allison. She kicked off her trainers and then removed her hoodie and joggers. She pulled out a pair of sandals from her backpack. She dropped them to the floor and slid her feet into them.

"And what did you tell them?"

"I told them what happened . . . duh," said Allison, rolling her eyes. She adjusted the black shorts she wore over her purple long-sleeved leotard.

This is getting me nowhere, thought Mia. *Think, think, think.*

"Did you see the local news? They covered the itching powder incident," said Mia. She pulled her hair up into a ponytail for the third time.

"Yup," said Allison. She then turned round and started to walk out of the locker room into the gym.

Mia jogged to chase after her. "Do you think they'll catch the person who did it?"

Allison stopped suddenly, causing Mia to bump into her.

"What is your problem, Hernandez? Give me some space," said Allison. She walked round Mia to go back into the locker area.

"What are you doing?" asked Mia.

"It's none of your business," said Allison. "But if you really must know, I forgot my water bottle. Is it okay with you if I get it?"

"Yeah, of course," said Mia. Her cheeks warmed from embarrassment. She wasn't very good at questioning suspects. She wanted to go back into the locker room to keep an eye on Allison, but she already had everything she needed. She walked as slowly as possible and kept looking over her shoulder.

If she takes much longer, then she is definitely up to something, thought Mia.

Mia heard footsteps behind her. When she spun round, she saw Allison walking towards her with the water bottle she had forgotten.

"Are you waiting for me or something?" asked Allison.

"No," lied Mia.

Allison shook her head and whispered, "Weirdo." Then she passed Mia and walked into the gym.

Coach Taylor asked all of the girls to sit in a circle on the floor exercise mat. She wanted to talk before warm-ups.

Mia looked round the circle. Most of the girls looked as tired as Mia felt. They were probably as sick as she was of responding to all the questions about their last two competitions. From the looks of it, Mia thought maybe she wasn't the only one who believed that someone from the Ridgefield Rams was to blame.

"It's been a really tough weekend," said Coach Taylor. "For all of us. I'm sure you saw the news. It looks like someone dumping itching powder into the chalk bins was the top story. I don't know about all of you, but my phone blew up after that."

The girls all nodded their heads and talked over each other.

"Yup!"

"Same!"

Coach held up her hands. "One at a time, girls. Riley, go ahead."

"Well, it started with people wanting first-hand details, seeing as I was there," said Riley. "Then, after the news, people started suggesting that it was someone on our team."

"Right," said Mia, nodding. "Especially since Ridgefield was at both meets and none of our girls were affected."

Mia looked at Allison, who casually took a sip from her water bottle.

"Yeah, I heard the same thing," Coach Taylor said. "I spent the weekend telling people that the music error was an unfortunate glitch. And that the itching powder was probably the work of Town Ridge Middle School's biggest class clown. I mean, that makes the most sense, right? But, you know, people love a conspiracy. We just have to shake it off."

"It's not that easy, Coach," said Mia. "Posts on my social media were brutal. People I thought were my friends called us cheaters."

"Yeah," said Riley. "And then people I didn't even know started trolling me. They said they were going to get back at us and we'd better watch out."

Lots of girls nodded their heads to say they had had similar experiences.

"I'm sorry that happened," said Coach. "There is absolutely no evidence to suggest that someone from Ridgefield is responsible for what happened at those meets."

"True," said Mia. "But now the accusation is out there."

I should say something, thought Mia. *Now is the perfect time.*

Mia took a deep breath. "To be honest, Coach, some of us even believe it."

Coach looked shocked, but some girls nodded in agreement with Mia.

"What?" asked Coach. She shifted in her seat, like she was nervous or uncomfortable. "You really think that someone from Ridgefield is responsible? That someone in this circle is sabotaging other teams to help us win?"

"I don't know," said Mia quietly. "But it's possible. Some people hate to lose so much, they're willing to do whatever it takes to win."

Mia looked around the circle. Some of her teammates stared at her with wide eyes. Others, though, nodded again.

So I'm not the only one who thinks one of us could have done it, Mia thought. When her gaze reached Allison, the two stared each other down.

"Okay," Coach said with a heavy sigh. "Today, we need to rebuild our trust in one another. You will work with a partner, doing exercises that require two people."

Mia and Riley, who were sitting next to each other, fist-bumped.

"You do not get to choose your own partner," said Coach. "I will match you."

Anyone but Allison, Mia pleaded silently. *Please, anyone!*

"Mia, you will team up with Allison."

Mia turned to Riley. "I think Coach hates me," she whispered.

Riley laughed. "Good luck," she said quietly. "Maybe you can get something out of her while you're working together."

"Maybe," said Mia. "If we don't kill each other first."

Once all of the girls were paired, Coach instructed them on what to do.

"The first exercise is the one-armed partner plank. Start by standing side by side. Now, both of you get down onto the mat in the plank position. When you're ready, the person on the right will put her left arm across her partner's back."

Allison lifted her arm and placed it across Mia's back.

"Then, the girl on the left will put her right arm across her partner's back."

"Easy," said Allison. "Don't knock me over."

"I'm not going to knock you over," said Mia.

"Hold the one-armed plank position, with your other arm on your partner for support, for as long as you can," said Coach. "Talk to each other. Make sure the other person is okay. If one is getting tired, tell the other person. Don't just drop out of the hold or else the other person will go down too."

"Are you okay?" asked Mia.

"Fine," said Allison. "You?"

"Fine," said Mia.

After a bit, Mia's arm started to shake, and Allison scrunched her eyes tight.

"You okay?" asked Mia. "Remember to breathe."

Instead of breathing, Allison yelled. "Agggghhh! It hurts!"

"Yeah, it does," said Mia. "My arm is shaking. I need to stop."

"Okay," said Allison. "You go first."

Mia slowly removed her arm from Allison's back and collapsed to the floor. Allison did the same.

"Okay, now one partner will be in a plank. Then the other should stand on one side down by their partner's ankles. When you're ready, jump over your partner's body, back and forth. Again, you'll need to talk to each other to find out if one person is getting tired and needs to stop."

"You'd better not fall on me, Hernandez," said Allison.

"I'm not going to fall on you," said Mia.

I don't trust you, and I think you're up to something, but I'm not going to fall on you, she thought.

"Do you really think I would fall on you on purpose?" asked Mia.

Maybe Allison has trust issues, she thought, hopping over Allison's body.

"I don't know," said Allison. "Maybe."

Mia hopped over Allison again.

"Do you really think I would sabotage other gymnastics teams?" Allison asked.

Mia was about to jump again but stopped. "I never said that."

"You didn't have to," said Allison. "What you said when we were in the circle made it clear that you think it's me."

Mia kept hopping back and forth over Allison's planked body until Coach told them to stop. Neither girl called it quits.

Allison dropped to the mat and then rolled onto her back. Mia reached her arm down and offered

Allison her hand. Allison grabbed Mia's hand and pulled herself up.

"Nice work, everyone," said Coach. "Now, let's get back to gymnastics."

Before the girls headed off to separate areas of the gym, Allison said, "You didn't answer my question. Do you really think I could do that?"

Mia paused for a moment. "I don't know," she finally said. "Maybe."

CHAPTER 7

WHEN THE BAR BREAKS

Coach Taylor stood on a bench in their locker room and raised her hands to get the girls' attention.

She put a finger to her lips. "Shhh! Listen . . ."

Muffled cheers from the crowd outside could be heard from the locker room.

"The place is packed," said Coach. "I didn't expect any less. Not only are we competing against our rivals, but people are interested to see me coach against my former coach. Normally, I'd say something like don't worry about winning or losing. Just do your best. I'll be honest, though – I'd love to beat her today."

The girls erupted in claps and cheers. Coach jumped down and everyone put their arms in the centre of a circle. "Ridgefield on three," she said. "One, two, three –"

"Ridgefield!" the girls shouted. Then they walked in a single-file line out of the locker room.

Thunderous applause greeted Mia and her teammates as they entered the gym. Parents and friends had filled the stands. One side wore Ridgefield's colours, blue and gold. The other side sported Brookfield's red and black. Being in their own training centre against their biggest rivals gave Mia and her teammates an extra boost of confidence.

After warm-ups, Mia, Riley and Allison were among the girls assigned to floor exercise first. Mia started the girls off. Her routine was upbeat to match her power tumbling passes. The music started with no problems. Mia lifted up on her toes and then powered across the mat for her first pass. She twisted slightly and put her hands down to go into a roundoff.

As soon as she landed, she threw herself up and backwards. Her legs sailed over and around, once, then twice, for two no-handed back handsprings. She landed with a boom – no wobbles. She threw her hands into the air and continued with her leaps, turns and remaining tumbling passes.

At the end of her routine, Mia ran off the mat to her teammates. They swallowed her in hugs and gave her high fives. Allison wasn't as enthusiastic, but she did manage to say, "Well done". Things were still tense between them.

When the judges posted her score, 9.6, Mia was happy. The team needed every tenth of a point they could get if they wanted to beat Brookfield.

Mia relaxed and watched everyone else compete. She was happy that the music was playing perfectly and the chalk wasn't making anyone itch, sneeze or wheeze.

It was the Brookfield team's turn on the uneven bars. Mia had been practising her new dismount, and she was getting better. Coach said it was up to her when to do it in competition. She didn't want to force her if she didn't feel ready. *Maybe I'll do it today,* thought Mia. *We might need the extra points.*

Mia watched as one of the Brookfield girls started her routine. She used a springboard to mount onto the low bar. She went into a glide kip with her legs together and then pushed up into a straddle, followed by a handstand. She did another glide kip and rotation round the bar. This move ended with a quick squat, with both of her feet on the low bar.

From here, she leaped forward to catch the high bar. As soon as her hands gripped the high bar, a deafening bang and screech filled the air. The bar collapsed and the gymnast crashed down onto the mat. Gasps filled the air as coaches and officials raced to the uneven bars area. The gymnast stood but then stumbled again. Her coach told her to stay seated until a medic was called.

"I can't believe this," Mia said to Riley.

The gym remained in shocked silence while the gymnast was checked. She didn't seem seriously hurt – more shocked than anything. She was still taken out in a wheelchair and sent to the hospital for a full evaluation.

Riley hugged Mia. "It's like we're cursed or something."

Mia pulled away. "Come on, Riley. You think this was another coincidence? Bad luck?"

"It could be," said Riley. "The bars are held together by bolts and wires. Bolts come loose. The tension could have been off. These things have happened before."

"This is the third incident, though," said Mia. She looked at Allison and added, "This was no accident."

When the judges announced that the competition would have to be rescheduled, Mia saw Allison race to the locker room.

"I'll be right back," said Mia. She ran after Allison. When she got there, she saw they were alone in the locker room.

"It was you! I know it!" said Mia.

"You're crazy, Mia," said Allison. She pulled out her clothes from her locker and started to get dressed out of her leotard. "I was standing next to you the whole time. How could it be me?"

"You probably offered to help check the equipment before Brookfield got here. You must have loosened the tension just enough so that it would look like an accident."

"Leave me alone," said Allison.

"So, you're not denying it," said Mia. "I wasn't positive at first with the music and the itching powder, but now I know for sure. You could have messed with the beam or the vault, but you chose the uneven bars because of me. You know I have a fear of flying off the bars. You taunted me for two years after I balked. You tampered with the bars to mess with my head even more and set up Brookfield to fail."

Allison was ready to leave. "Get out of my way."

Mia stood firm, waiting and hoping Allison would finally admit to it.

But instead of confessing, Allison shouted, "Move!" and pushed past Mia.

Riley and the other girls poured into the locker room then.

"Are you okay?" asked Riley. "What's going on?"

"It's her. I know it is," said Mia. "I need to find Coach Taylor."

CHAPTER 8

A CONFESSION

Mia texted her mum, who was sitting in the stands, and told her not to wait. She would walk the short distance home later. Mia quickly put on her joggers, long-sleeved T-shirt and trainers.

Then she bolted out of the locker room and started looking for Coach Taylor. Mia became more frantic as she saw Brookfield gymnasts, angry and crying. Many were being comforted by their families and friends.

She hurt so many people! Mia thought. *I can't let her get away with it. I have to find Coach!*

Mia waited until the gym and locker room were almost empty. Coach had to be either outside or in her office. She raced through the front door and circled the building to see if she was talking to officials, parents or the press outside. No sign of her. Mia entered the empty training centre, wondering how she could have missed her. Then again, the place was packed.

I guess the best thing I could do now is text her and tell her I need to talk to her as soon as possible.

Mia pulled out her mobile phone to text Coach Taylor. News of the incident was already spreading on social media. The accusations were worse than last time. People were convinced that someone on the Ridgefield team was to blame.

Unfortunately, they're right, thought Mia. *One of the Ridgefield Rams is to blame!*

Mia jogged across the gym towards Coach Taylor's office, which was tucked away in another part of the building. As she got closer, she heard Coach and another woman arguing. Mia peeked round the corner and into the office. The other woman was the Brookfield coach, Eliza Jones.

"You're not fooling me, Lauren," said Coach Jones. "I warned the Ridgefield principal not to hire you. I told her about your past, but she was convinced that you had grown up. She said the choices you made in high school were ancient history. I knew better. I knew it. You've always been obsessed with winning. The lights going out and the fire alarm being set off when you were on my team – that was you. I'm sure of it."

"You could never prove that," said Coach Taylor. "But I got punished for it anyway."

"You're right, Lauren," said Coach Jones. "I couldn't prove it, but that's why I didn't make you captain. That's why you were eventually kicked off the team. You became a toxic teammate, poisoning everyone around you instead of lifting them up."

Say something, Coach, Mia thought. *This can't be true.*

"And now I know I was right," said Coach Jones. "You come back after all these years and the pranks start all over again. History is repeating itself, and it's all because of you."

Mia took a deep breath and was about to jump into the conversation to tell both of them that Allison was to blame.

Just then Coach Taylor said, "You're right, Eliza. I took this job to get back at you and everyone else in this region who ruined my gymnastics career. I could have been an elite athlete, but my reputation was ruined after you kicked me off the team."

What is she talking about? Mia thought.

"None of the athletic clubs would take me, and that destroyed my chances of being in top shape for college. So, yes, I came back to coach the state champions to another title. That really wasn't enough, though. I wanted to twist the knife, so to speak."

Mia held back a gasp.

"So I switched the music. I put the itching powder in the chalk bins, and I loosened the tension on the bars. Maybe now you will all think twice before messing with me!"

Mia emerged from the shadows, her mouth hanging open.

"Mia –" Coach Taylor started.

Mia put her hand up to stop her, a move Coach often used. "Save it. I've heard everything. Coach Jones, I will tell anyone who needs to hear it – the principal, the press, the entire gymnastics community – that Coach Taylor confessed to sabotaging those teams."

"I'm sorry," said Coach Jones. "You girls are fine athletes. You deserve a better coach."

"I agree," said Mia. Tears pricked the corners of her eyes. Then she looked at Coach Taylor. "We trusted you," she said.

Coach Jones called the Ridgefield principal and

asked her to come to the training centre straight away. As promised, Mia stayed to explain what she had heard. Then Mia, Coach Jones and the Ridgefield principal watched as Coach Taylor packed up her personal belongings and left the gym for good.

CHAPTER 9

THE STATE CHAMPIONSHIP

Coach Bennett, the Ridgefield Rams previous gymnastics coach, came out of retirement to lead the girls through the rest of the season.

When she arrived at the first practice session after the Brookfield competition, the girls swallowed her in a group hug. She was what the team needed as they headed into their final weeks of the season.

Everyone now knew none of the girls were to blame. It was decided that their previous wins would stand. Now, all the gymnasts wanted was a chance to prove themselves fair and square.

The girls were hyped up on the bus ride to the state tournament held at the university. Everyone was ready to compete.

Mia walked under the bright lights of the big, fancy gym. She twirled around, in awe of all of the banners hanging on the walls. She imagined what it would be like to compete in high school and then college.

Once the girls were changed and ready to walk in, Mia turned to Coach Bennett. There was something she needed to do.

"Can I say something to the team before we go out?" she asked.

"Sure," said Coach.

Mia stood on a bench so that everyone could see and hear her.

"Before we go in there, I want to apologize to Allison for all of the horrible things I said about her," said Mia.

She looked around at her teammates. Then she made eye contact with Allison.

"I should have said something sooner," Mia continued, "but I was embarrassed and didn't know if you would ever forgive me. I understand if you don't, but I want you to know that I'm sorry."

A few of the girls nodded.

"Also, win or lose today, we're going to celebrate with a pizza party at my house," Mia finished. "My parents said it was okay. We've earned it."

The girls clapped and cheered as Mia jumped to the floor.

Allison smiled. "Thanks, Mia," she said. "I forgive you."

"Yeah?"

"Of course," said Allison, nodding. "I mean, you're still a weirdo, but we're teammates. We need to support each other, and we need to set an example, right?"

"Right," said Mia. "I guess Coach Taylor wasn't all bad after all. We did learn some valuable lessons from her."

"Now let's go and win this thing," said Allison.

* * *

As the day's competition played out, the Ridgefield Rams were in a tight battle for first place. Everything hinged on Mia's uneven bars routine.

The Ridgefield Rams could win their second state championship title. But Mia had to complete her new dismount, the double salto backward tuck, and stick the landing.

Mia waited for the judge's signal that they were ready. She took deep breaths and triple-checked her grips. When she got the signal, she raised her arms and jumped forwards.

She gripped the lower bar and ran through her routine. The bar squeaked and bent slightly with every move.

First up was a glide kip to handstand. Then a glide kip, stoop through, transition to top bar. Another kip cast to a handstand and then two clear hip circles to handstands. One giant circle backwards into a one-hundred-and eighty-degree turn into a handstand. One, two, three backward giant circles with straddled legs.

The air whooshed past her ears.

"You've got this!" yelled Allison.

I've got this, Mia told herself as she went through her routine. *Faith and physics.*

Mia came round the final time and let go. She flew into the air and flipped her body all the way around, legs pulled into a tuck. Once. Twice.

She landed with a thud on the mat, her knees bent and her arms out to steady her. No wobbles. She'd nailed it.

Mia threw her arms up and smiled wide. Tears of joy filled her eyes as she ran to her teammates.

When her score of 9.8 was posted, Mia and her teammates exploded. They were state champions again. And when Allison hugged her, Mia realized that she had something else to celebrate – a new friendship.

GLOSSARY

accusation act of saying that someone did something wrong

balk in gymnastics, when a gymnast develops a fear of a skill and stops before even attempting it

cast in gymnastics, when a gymnast moves her hips away from and then back to the bars

conspiracy secret, dishonest plan made by two or more people

dismount move done to get off an apparatus

embarrass cause someone else to feel shame

incident unexpected and often bad thing that happens

kip in gymnastics, a three-step move often used to mount the bars; a gymnast jumps forwards, grabs the bar, glides forwards, pikes her legs up to the bar and then pulls herself up onto the bar

momentum force or speed created by a movement

rivals teams competing for the same trophy or in the same area

sabotage damage, destroy or interfere on purpose

salto in gymnastics, when a gymnast does a flip in the air

DISCUSSION QUESTIONS

1. Coach Taylor shares the words of an ancient Chinese general, Sun Tzu: "Know thy enemy and know yourself; in a hundred battles, you will never be defeated." What do you think this means? Do you agree?

2. Mia and Allison are teammates, but they don't have a very friendly relationship. What makes a good friend? Can you be a good teammate to a person without being their friend?

3. Mia apologizes to Allison for accusing her of cheating. Talk about a time you apologized for something. How did it feel?

WRITING PROMPTS

1. Imagine Mia has a different outcome on the uneven bars. Write a new ending to the story. Do the Rams still win? How do the girls react?

2. Mia let fear affect her performance on the uneven bars. Write about a time something happened that made you fearful of trying something new. What did you do to overcome your fear?

3. Write a news story that covers the chalk powder switch incident.

ALL ABOUT GYMNASTICS

Gymnastics dates back to ancient Greece. It was one of the first sports in the Olympics. Women were not allowed to compete in gymnastics until the 1920s.

Gymnastics is a sport that combines strength, flexibility, balance and control. Women's gymnastics has four events: floor exercise, uneven bars, balance beam and vault. Men's gymnastics has six events: floor exercise, parallel bars, high bar, pommel horse, vault and rings.

In 1976, Romanian athlete Nadia Comaneci became the first gymnast in Olympic history to be awarded the perfect score of 10.0 for her performance on the uneven bars.

Max Whitlock is the most successful British male gymnast. He has so far won three gold and three bronze Olympic medals.

In 1996, Dominique Dawes became the first African American woman to win an individual gymnastics Olympic medal; she won bronze for her floor exercise routine. Dawes was also the first black woman of any nationality to win a gold medal in gymnastics (for team gold).

In 2012, Gabby Douglas became the first African American gymnast, and the first woman of colour of any nationality, to win the Olympic gold medal for the individual all-around. Douglas was also the first American woman to win both team and individual all-around gold medals at the same Olympics.

One of the most decorated gymnasts of all time is Simone Biles. She has a combined total of 32 Olympic and World Championship medals.

SOLVE ALL THE SPORT MYSTERIES!

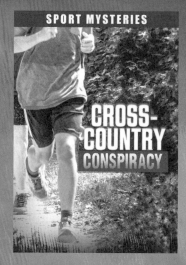

SPORT MYSTERIES

CROSS-COUNTRY
CONSPIRACY

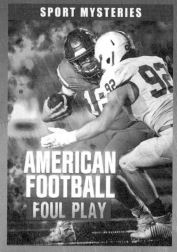

SPORT MYSTERIES

AMERICAN
FOOTBALL
FOUL PLAY

SPORT MYSTERIES

FULL-COURT
MESS

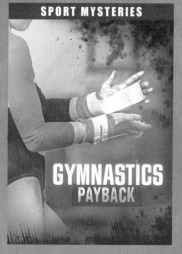

SPORT MYSTERIES

GYMNASTICS
PAYBACK

ABOUT THE AUTHOR

Cindy L. Rodriguez is an American author. She wrote the YA novel *When Reason Breaks* and is a contributor to the anthology *Life Inside My Mind: 31 Authors Share Their Personal Struggles*. She has also written *Volleyball Ace* and *Drill Team Determination*, other Raintree sport books. Before becoming a teacher, she was an award-winning newspaper reporter and researcher. Cindy is a big fan of the three Cs: coffee, chocolate and coconut. She is currently a middle school reading specialist in Connecticut, where she lives with her family.